MY FIRST STICKERS

Space

Have fun completing the activities
in this space-themed book!

✱

Use your pencils to color, doodle, and
complete the activities on each page.

✱

Where there is a missing sticker, you will see
an empty shape. Search your sticker pages
to find the missing sticker.

You can also press out some cool
characters and brilliant bookmarks
from your card pages.

make
believe
ideas

Astronaut adventure

Whoosh!

Join the dots to build the rocket ship.

Zoom!

Color the stars.

1 2 3 4 5 6 7 8 9 10 11 12 13 14 15 16 17 18 19 20

Solar system

Sticker the missing planets and stars to finish the solar system.

Can you find three aliens?

3

Super space

Sticker the missing circles and triangles to complete the space mission.

4

How many triangles can you see? Write the answer.

Awesome astronaut

Guide the astronaut across the moon maze to his rocket. Avoid the aliens.

Start

Finish

Tasty treats

Find the missing stickers, and then follow the lines to see each alien's favorite food.

8

Alien travels

Color the spaceship to match the one above.

What's different?

Find and circle five differences between the scenes.

12

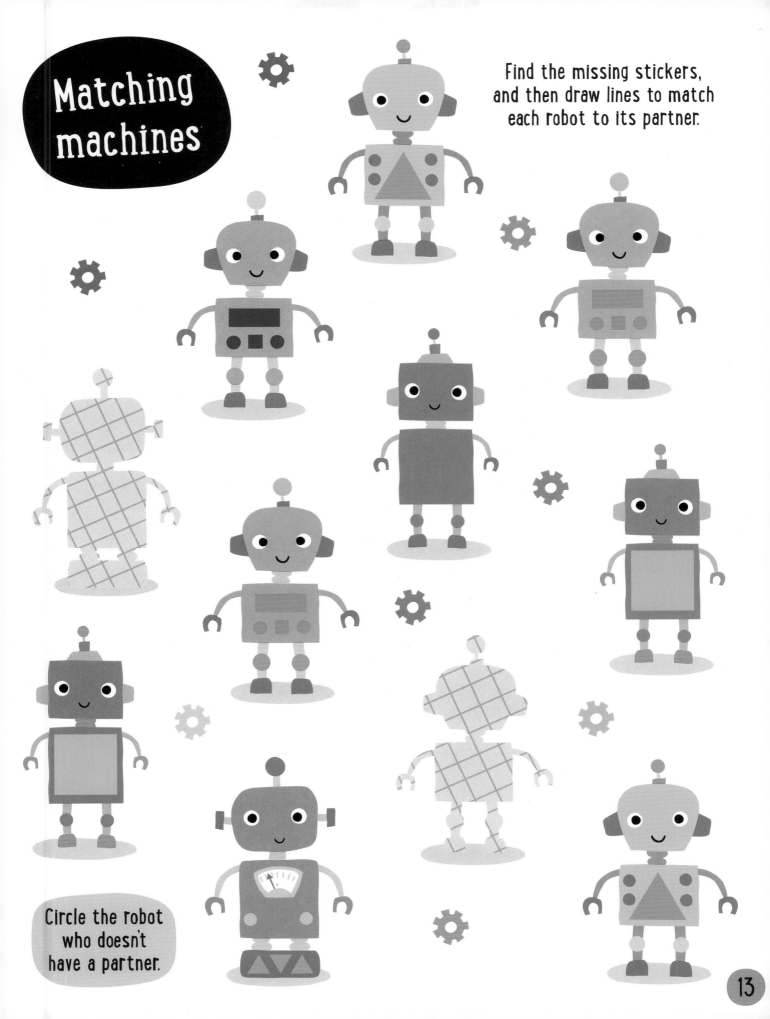

Matching machines

Find the missing stickers, and then draw lines to match each robot to its partner.

Circle the robot who doesn't have a partner.

Space rows

Use stickers and color to complete the space rows.

 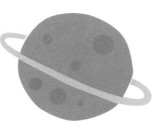 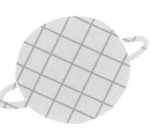 

  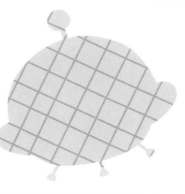 

Weird creatures

Copy and color the aliens. Use the grids to guide you.

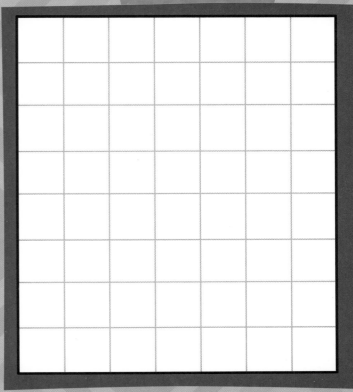

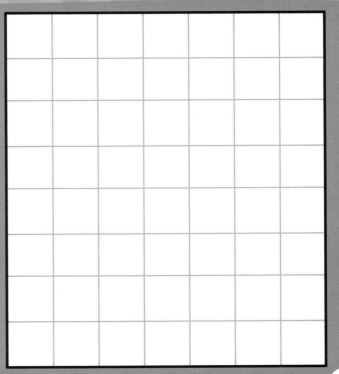

Flying home

Find the missing stickers, and then trace the rocket's trail.

Draw an astronaut in the window!

Hanging in outer space

Press out the space shapes
and shade the reverse sides.
Then, thread some ribbon
through the holes and hang
them wherever you like!

Super space bookmarks

Press out the super space bookmarks and decorate them with your stickers.